COUNTING

is

SIMPLY BEAUTIFUL

by

Cheri Alphonse Hayes

Illustrations by Gennel Marie Sollano

To order additional copies of this book, contact:
Xlibris
844-714-8691
www.Xlibris.com
Orders@Xlibris.com

ISBN: Softcover   978-1-6641-4486-6
       EBook   978-1-6641-4485-9

Print information available on the last page

Rev. date: 02/23/2021

Dedicated to the...

Sons and daughters of our isle; my love for you
I can't deny. Take this book and hold it dear;
whether you are far or near. Each page is filled with
you and me; in current times and history.

Special thanks to
Lauraine "Freca" Barnard and Albertha Ellis

1 one
yonn

One bright sun...
cascading the land; through hills
and valleys, beaches and sand.

2 two
dé

Two majestic pitons...
courageously tall; a symbol so
grand on an island so small.

3 three
twa

Three coconut trees...
no season to bear; awaiting the
pickers, I sure hope they share!

4 **four** kat

Four sailboats...
on the ocean blue; where are they
heading, I haven't a clue.

5 five
senk

Five fish fly...
above the water; looks like mother,
father, baby, son and daughter.

6 six
sis

Six fisherman...
casts their nets with weights; hoping
to fill, their big wooden crates.

7 seven
sèt

Seven parasailers...
fly high above; admiring the view we
naturally love.

8 eight
ywit

Eight coasters wait...
to be filled for a tour; promising
excitement, it won't be a bore.

9 nine
nèf

Nine vendors...
line the streets with their wares;
they're all authentic, I do declare!

10 ten dis

Ten cultural sights...
lie ahead; they are-in-all
the books that I have read.

11 eleven
wonz

Eleven coins and dollars...
to spend or save; can you guess
the decision I made?

12 twelve douz

Cane

Golden Apple

Sour orange

Seawet

Mango

Sourso[p]

Guava

Sorrel

Starfruit

Tamarind

Lime

Passion fruit

Twelve drinks...
all locally made; enjoy them in the
sun or the shade.

13

December

SUN	MON	TUE	WED	THU	FRI	SAT
		1	2	3	4	5
6	7	8	9	10	11	12
▲	14	15	16	17	18	19
20	21	22	23	24	25	26
27	28	29	30	31		

Thirteen is the day in December...
our National Day we do remember.

14

fourteen
katòz

Fourteen flowers...
in full bloom; removing
every trace of gloom

Chenille

Ginger Lily

Bird of Paradise

Bougainvillea

Heliconia

Christmas Candle

Parrot's Beak

Buttercups

Bleeding Hearts

Hibiscus

Red Ixora

Bread and Cheese

La Marguerite

Red Anthurium Lily

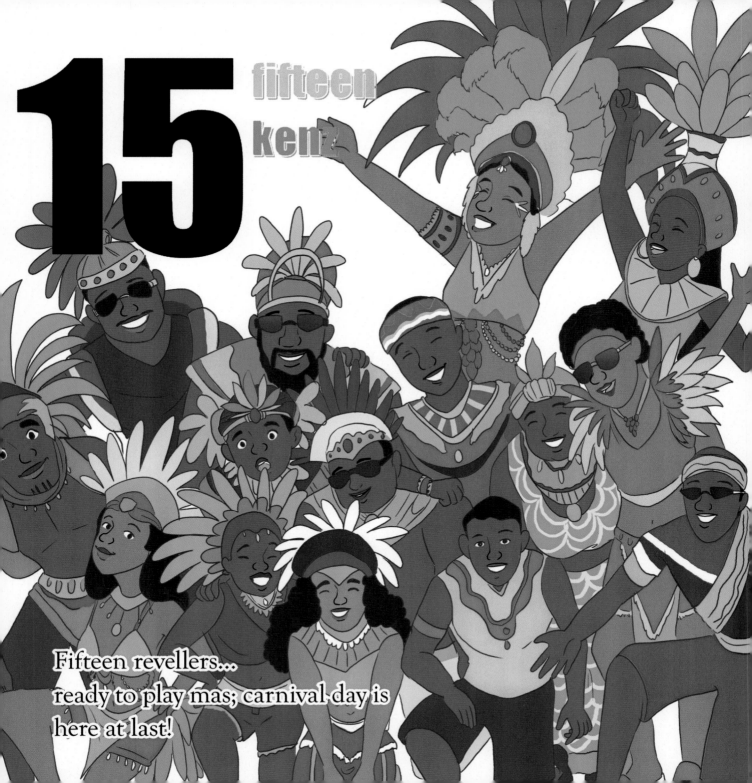

15 fifteen
kenz

Fifteen revellers...
ready to play mas; carnival day is
here at last!

Sixteen children...
walk to school; they've all
been taught the Golden Rule.

17

seventeen

disèt

Vive La Marguerite!

Seventeen dancers...
in the streets; all chanting Vive
La Marguerite!

18 eighteen dizwit

Eighteen police...
march in the band; royal and loyal
to the land

19
nineteen
diznèf

Nineteen places...
family-filled; to see them all
is truly a thrill.

Gros Islet • • Cas en Bas

Monchy •

Dauphin •

Castries • Grand Anse •

Marigot Bay •

La Caye •

Anse la Raye • Dennery •

Canaries •

Praslin •

Soufriere • • Mon Repos

• Micoud

Desruisseaux

Choiseul •

Laborie •
Vieux Fort •

Caribbean Sea

Atlantic Ocean

20 twenty
ven

Virginia Alexander
Choreographer

George Charles
Chief Minister

John Compton
Prime Minister

Gerald Cyril
Policeman

Marie "Sesenne" Desca
Cultural Dancer

Jeff "Pelay" Elva
Musician

Dawn French
Author

Ronald "Boo" Hinkson
Musician

Edward "Chef Harry" Joseph
Chef

Arthur Lewis
Economist

Twenty leaders...
then and now; paving the way and
making us proud.

Pearlette Louisy
Governor General

Joseph Marcell
Actor

Francis "Mindoo" Phillip
Cricketer

Carmen Rene
Educator

Levern Spencer
High Jumper

Dunstan St. Omer
Artist

Antoine Theodore
Pharmacist

Dexter Theodore
Lawyer

George Theophilus
Banker

Derek Walcott
Poet

Spreading love throughout the land;
together as one we always stand.
Setting goals and fulfilling the mission;
claiming our rights as St. Lucians!

Printed in the United States
By Bookmasters